by Tracey West

Scholastic Inc.
New York • Toronto • London • Auckland • Sydney
Mexico City • New Delhi • Hong Kong • Buenos Aires

ISBN 0-439-33228-1

Published by Scholastic Inc. All rights reserved.

SCHOLASTIC and associated logos are trademarks and/or registered trademarks of Scholastic Inc.

Cover and interior illustrations by Bill Alger

Designed by Mark Neston

12 11 10 9 8 7 6 5 4 3 2 2 3 4 5 6 7/0

Printed in the U.S.A.

First Scholastic printing, January 2002

Read This First!

Sugar...spice...and everything nice...

These were the ingredients chosen to create the perfect little girl. But Professor Utonium accidentally added an extra ingredient to the concoction—Chemical X!

And thus, The Powerpuff Girls were born! Using their ultra superpowers, Blossom, Bubbles, and Buttercup have dedicated their lives to fighting crime and the forces of evil!

But now, The Powerpuff Girls need your help! In every Pick a Powerpuff Path, *you will take on the role of one of the characters and help save the day.*

In this adventure, you will be Bubbles, the sweet (but hard-core) Powerpuff Girl, as she and her sisters, Blossom and Buttercup, search for Petunia the elephant, who has disappeared from Fred Friendly's Circus. You will choose what Bubbles will do as The Powerpuff Girls try to get Petunia back to the circus before show time! The story will be different depending on the choices you make. After you choose a path, follow along to continue the story.

When you're done, you can start over and make new choices to read a completely different story.

So what are you waiting for? There's an elephant on the loose!

The city of Townsville! On most days, The Powerpuff Girls are busy fighting crime. But today they were thinking about something else....

"Who is going to Fred Friendly's Circus this weekend?" asked Ms. Keane, The Powerpuff Girls' teacher at Pokey Oaks Kindergarten.

"We are! We are!" shouted The Powerpuff Girls.

Blossom, Bubbles, and Buttercup were so excited. They had never been to a circus before.

"I can't wait to see the ringmaster," said Blossom.

"I can't wait to see the high-flying daredevils!" said Buttercup.

"I can't wait to see all the nice animals," said Bubbles.

Ms. Keane smiled. "Fred Friendly's is a special circus," she said. "The animals who perform there were rescued by Fred. Many of them had been mistreated. Now they live on Fred Friendly's farm. Fred holds special circus shows to raise money to help save more animals."

"What kinds of animals are there?" asked Bubbles. She liked animals a lot. She could even talk to animals, thanks to her superpowers.

"Well, there is a lion. And a trained snake," said Ms. Keane. "And I think the star of the show is—"

"Petunia the elephant is missing!"

A man in a bright orange suit and a big bow tie burst into the classroom. He looked upset.

"Fred Friendly," said Ms. Keane. "What are you doing here?"

"I need The Powerpuff Girls to help me," said Fred Friendly. "Petunia the elephant is missing from the circus. She's my star act! We can't do a show without her. Besides, I'm worried about her."

Bubbles flew out of her seat. "We'll find your elephant, Mr. Friendly," she said. "Don't worry."

"Right!" said Blossom. "Come on, Girls. Let's go to the circus!"

Blossom, Bubbles, and Buttercup whizzed out the window. In seconds, they landed on the circus grounds. Many colorful tents dotted the area. Clowns, acrobats, and many other performers were scurrying around, getting ready for the show.

Blossom had an idea. "It's a good thing you can talk to animals, Bubbles. Maybe some of the circus animals know what happened to Petunia."

"Yeah," said Buttercup. "No one can get into the mind of an elephant like you can. You should lead this mission."

"Right," said Blossom. "So where should we start, Bubbles?"

Bubbles thought for a minute. "Ms. Keane said there was a lion and a snake. I can start with one of them!"

If Bubbles talks to the snake first, turn to page 8.

If Bubbles talks to the lion first, turn to page 11.

A clown with curly green hair walked past.

"Excuse me, mister," said Bubbles. "Is there a snake around here?"

The clown pointed to a yellow tent. "Over there," said the clown. He shivered. "But I wouldn't go in there if I were you. That snake gives me the creeps."

"We're not afraid of some slimy serpent!" said Buttercup.

The Girls flew to the tent and stepped inside. A huge python was curled up on a pile of satin pillows. Shiny brown-and-gold scales covered its long body.

Bubbles used her superpowers to talk to the snake.

"*Hello, Mr. Snake,*" she said.

The snake flicked the tip of his long tail. "*Call me Sssal,*" the snake hissed.

"*My name is Bubbles,*" Bubbles continued. "*My sisters, Blossom and Buttercup, and I are looking for Petunia the elephant. Do you know where she is?*"

"*Yesss,*" Sal hissed. "*I sssaw that sssilly elephant following a trail of peanutsss thisss morning. Petunia lovesss peanutsss.*"

Sal motioned toward the door of the tent. Outside, Bubbles saw peanuts on the ground.

Bubbles thanked Sal. Then she told her sisters what the snake had said. The Girls flew out of the tent. They followed the trail of peanuts.

Suddenly, a black seal blocked their path.

"*Stop!*" said the seal. "*Don't listen to that snake. He's a liar!*"

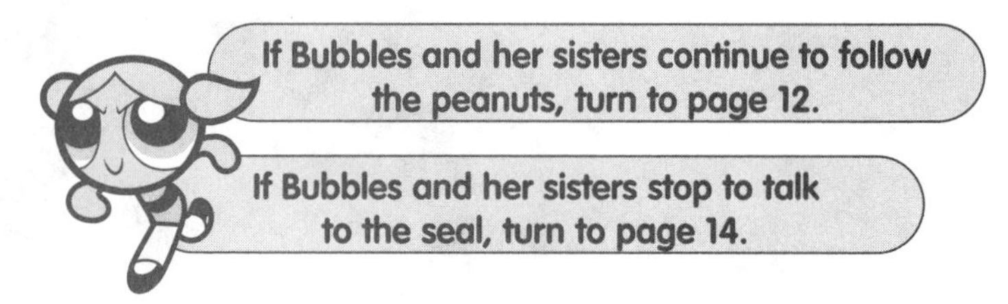

Bubbles heard a loud roar coming from a red tent nearby.

"I bet the lion is in there," Bubbles said. She flew toward the tent with her sisters behind her.

Bubbles used her superpowers to talk to the lion.

"*Hi there,*" Bubbles said. "*My name is Bubbles.*"

"*I'm Lenny,*" said the lion. He lifted one of his front paws and scratched behind his fluffy golden mane.

Bubbles explained that they were looking for Petunia the elephant.

"*We thought you might know something,*" she said.

"*I'm not sure what happened to Petunia,*" said Lenny. "*But I know she was upset about something. I think she may have run away. I bet she went to the park. She really likes trees and flowers and stuff.*"

Bubbles told her sisters what the lion had said.

"Maybe we should find Petunia's trainer," suggested Blossom. "He might know more about this."

"We're wasting time," said Buttercup. "Let's go look for Petunia in the park."

"Those are both good ideas," said Bubbles. "I'm not sure what to do."

If Bubbles decides she and her sisters should talk to Petunia's trainer, turn to page 15.

If Bubbles decides to go to the park, turn to page 22.

"*Sal seemed perfectly nice to me,*" Bubbles told the seal. "*I believe his story.*"

The seal shrugged. "*Okay, do as you like, but don't say I didn't warn you.*"

The Girls flew above the trail of peanuts. Suddenly, Bubbles knocked into something hard. It was a clear plastic wall. The Girls had flown right into it!

Bubbles slid to the ground. The grass and dirt gave way underneath her.

"We're falling!" Bubbles yelled.

It all happened so fast. Bubbles landed in the dirt. Blossom and Buttercup landed next to her. They had fallen into a hole in the ground!

"It's a trap!" Buttercup fumed.

Slam! The Girls looked up. A heavy metal lid covered the hole above them.

"I'm sorry," Bubbles said. "I guess the seal was right."

Bubbles's eyes adjusted to the darkness. To the right, she saw a tunnel leading...well, somewhere. It could be a way out. Above, the metal lid blocked their way. But they might be able to blast through it.

"Looks like we've got two ways to go," said Blossom.

"But which way is best?" Bubbles wondered.

If Bubbles and her sisters decide to blast through the metal lid, turn to page 16.

If they go through the tunnel, turn to page 18.

"*Why do you say that Sal is a liar?*" Bubbles asked the seal.

"*Sal is the slipperiest character in the whole circus,*" the seal said. "*Just last week we were playing cards, and Sal cheated.*"

"That may be so," Blossom said. "But why would he send us off on a wild-goose chase after Petunia?"

After Bubbles had translated Blossom's words, the seal replied, "*I'm not sure. But someone came to see the snake early this morning. I couldn't see whoever it was well enough to give you a good description, but it was someone pretty short. After the visitor left, I saw Sal plant this trail of peanuts.*"

"Maybe Sal is in league with one of Townsville's villains," guessed Blossom.

"Mojo Jojo and Princess Morbucks are both shrimps," Buttercup pointed out.

"Maybe we should go talk to them," Bubbles agreed.

If Bubbles and her sisters fly to Princess Morbucks's house, turn to page 20.

If The Powerpuff Girls fly to Mojo Jojo's observatory, turn to page 25.

The Girls decided that talking to Petunia's trainer was a good idea. They found him in a small trailer.

Barney the trainer was a tall, thin man with messy brown hair. He was blowing his nose.

"I don't understand what happened to Petunia," Barney sobbed. "She was happy here. I know she was. She wouldn't have run away. Somebody must have kidnapped her!"

Barney picked up a picture of Petunia from his desk. "Oh, Petunia. I miss you so much!"

"Something's not right here," Blossom whispered to her sisters. "The lion said that Petunia was definitely not happy. Maybe we need to snoop around some."

"But the lion also said he thought Petunia went to the park," insisted Buttercup.

If Bubbles agrees to snoop around Barney's trailer, turn to page 21.

If Bubbles and her sisters decide to look for Petunia in the park, turn to page 22.

"Let's blast through that lid!" Bubbles said.

"All together, Girls!" cried Blossom.

Zap! Pink laser eye beams shot from Blossom's eyes.

Zap! Blue laser eye beams shot from Bubbles's eyes.

Zap! Green laser eye beams shot from Buttercup's eyes.

Boom! The blast hit the metal lid, sending it shooting into the air... and right into a group of clowns walking by!

The Girls flew out of the hole. The clowns had been knocked off of their big red feet. The Girls helped the clowns get back up.

"Sorry," said Bubbles. "We didn't know you were there."

Then Bubbles noticed something about one of the clowns. He was tall and skinny with a mop of red hair. Bubbles was sure she knew that clown.

It was Rainbow! The clown was once a villain called Mr. Mime. He stole all the color from Townsville. Of course, The Powerpuff Girls had defeated him and tossed him in jail. What was he doing in Fred Friendly's Circus?

Before Bubbles could say anything, Blossom nudged her. "I found this outside the hole," she said. "It's a clue."

Blossom held up a gold wrench engraved with the initials P.M.

"P.M.? It must belong to Princess Morbucks!" said Buttercup.

Bubbles's head was spinning. Should they follow Rainbow—or go find Princess right away?

If Bubbles decides she and her sisters should follow Rainbow the Clown, turn to page 43.

If Bubbles decides she and her sisters should go to Princess's house, turn to page 20.

"Let's try the tunnel," said Bubbles. "Maybe it will lead us to Petunia."

Blossom and Buttercup agreed. The three sisters floated through the dark tunnel. Bubbles used her blue laser eye beams to light the way.

Soon Bubbles saw a strange shape heading toward them.

It was some sort of creature with soft, gray fur. It was bigger than Professor Utonium and had whiskers on the end of its pointy snout. It looked just like...

"A giant mole!" cried Bubbles. She wondered whether the creature was an animal or a monster. If the giant mole was an animal, she could try to talk to him. If he was a monster, she'd probably have to attack him.

If Bubbles tries to talk to the mole, turn to page 24.

If Bubbles attacks the mole, turn to page 26.

Bubbles turned to Petunia. "*Can you help us out with a water attack?*" she asked the elephant.

Petunia didn't hesitate. She dipped her trunk in the trough of water in her cage. Then she squirted a wave of water at the robot.

Sizzle! Pop! Phhht! The water blew out the robot's electric circuits. Sparks flew from the robot.

"No fair! No fair!" Princess screamed. She angrily pressed every control button on the panel, but it was no use.

"*Good work, Petunia!*" Bubbles cheered.

Blossom and Buttercup flew into the air.

"We're back and better than ever!" shouted Buttercup.

"Let's go see what Princess is up to," Bubbles decided.

The Girls flew to Princess Morbucks's mansion. The big, white house seemed to go on for miles.

Princess's daddy had more money than anyone else in the world. But that hadn't made Princess happy. She always seemed to want things she couldn't have. And she got them any way she could.

Once, Princess's daddy had used his money to buy Princess a contraption so she could be a superhero, just like The Powerpuff Girls. But Princess didn't really want to help anybody—just herself. The Girls had stopped Princess from becoming a superhero. And Princess had been trying to get revenge ever since.

The Girls landed at the mansion's gates. All was quiet. There was no sign of Princess.

If Bubbles rings Princess's buzzer, turn to page 27.

If Bubbles and her sisters blast their way into the mansion, turn to page 28.

"It couldn't hurt to snoop around a little," whispered Bubbles.

The Girls said good-bye to Barney and left the trailer. Then they hid behind some bushes and waited for Barney to leave as well. As soon as he was gone, the Girls flew through the window back into the trailer.

Pictures of Petunia were plastered on the walls. Peanut shells littered the floor.

The Girls looked everywhere. They looked under Barney's desk. They leafed through his papers. Buttercup even picked up the rug and looked under there. But there was nothing unusual in the trailer.

Then Blossom spotted a piece of paper on the floor and picked it up.

"Is it about Petunia?" asked Bubbles.

"Not really," said Blossom. "It's a letter from the Nutty Brand peanut company. They're thanking Barney for switching his brand of peanuts."

Buttercup frowned. "I told you we were wasting our time here. Let's look in the park already!"

If Bubbles and her sisters decide it's time to go to the park to look for Petunia, turn to page 22.

If Bubbles and her sisters stay at the circus to question some more animals, turn to page 31.

"Okay, let's try the park!" Bubbles said.

The Girls flew toward the park. Bubbles was starting to feel nervous. This search was taking a lot longer than she thought it would. She hoped they'd find Petunia before the circus performance started!

As they flew over the park, Bubbles noticed that something was wrong. Bushes and flowers were crushed. Picnic lunches were scattered across the grass.

"It looks like a hurricane hit this place!" cried Buttercup.

"Or maybe an elephant," said Blossom.

Then Bubbles noticed something else. Five boys were hanging around the monkey bars.

Five *green* boys.

"It's the Gangreen Gang!" shouted Bubbles. Maybe Petunia hadn't stomped through the park after all.

The Girls zipped over to the boys.

"Did you green goof-ups wreck the park?" Buttercup asked them.

Ace, their leader, cackled. "You're barking up the wrong tree this time, gals. We didn't do this. An elephant did!"

"Yeah," chimed in Big Billy. "It went thataway." He pointed across the park.

Bubbles wasn't sure what to do. The Gangreen Gang had never told the truth before. But how could they have known about Petunia?

"Now get outta here!" said Ace. "This park is Gangreen Gang territory."

If Bubbles and her sisters decide to pound the truth out of the Gangreen Gang, turn to page 36.

If Bubbles and her sisters believe the Gangreen Gang and don't attack them, turn to page 32.

Bubbles greeted the giant mole. "*Hello there,*" she said. "*Did you see an elephant come through here?*"

The mole's whiskers twittered. "*I don't know what an elephant is,*" squeaked the mole. "*But I did see a little girl down here. She dug that hole over there. Then she ran down the tunnel. She was going so fast she didn't even see me.*"

"*Thanks, Mr. Mole,*" Bubbles said.

Bubbles told her sisters what the mole had said. Buttercup seemed surprised that the mole was so friendly.

"Why should we believe a mutant mole?" she asked.

"I don't see why he would lie to Bubbles," said Blossom.

Buttercup nodded. "You're right. Let's go!"

"Besides," added Blossom, "I have a hunch who that little girl is..."

Continue on page 34.

"Let's see what Mojo Jojo is up to," suggested Bubbles.

Blossom and Buttercup agreed. The Girls flew off to Mojo Jojo's lair. The evil monkey lived in an observatory on top of Townsville Volcano Mountain, where he was constantly planning to destroy The Powerpuff Girls or rule the world, whichever came first.

The Girls flew into the top window. Mojo Jojo was humming and polishing his giant laser machine. He jumped when he saw the Girls.

"Powerpuff Girls!" cried Mojo Jojo. "What are you doing here?"

"We're looking for Petunia the elephant," Bubbles said. "Did you take her?"

"An elephant!" replied the shocked monkey. "There is no elephant here. What would I, Mojo Jojo, do with an elephant? I am here in my observatory and there is no elephant with me."

Bubbles looked around. There was no sign of Petunia anywhere. Was Mojo telling the truth?

If Bubbles believes Mojo and decides she and her sisters should go to Princess's mansion instead, turn to page 20.

If Bubbles decides to question Mojo further, turn to page 33.

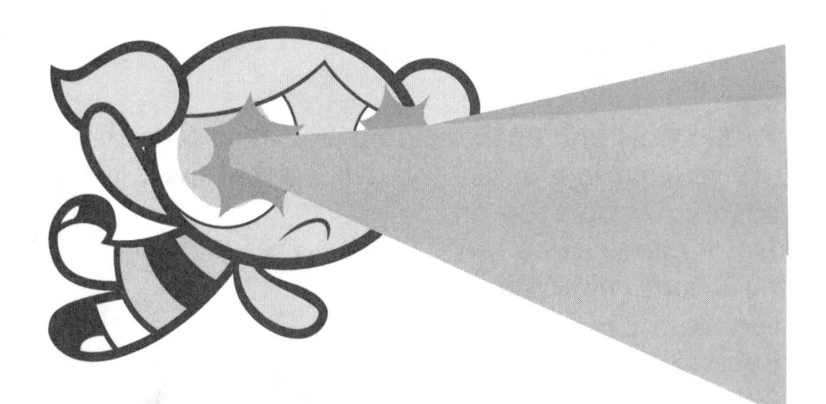

Blue laser eye beams shot out of Bubbles's eyes. The eye beams zapped the mole and sent it flying backward.

"*That wasn't very nice!*" squeaked the mole.

"What are you gonna do about it?" Buttercup replied, after Bubbles translated.

There was a low rumbling sound. Bubbles turned and looked behind her. Five more giant moles were crawling out of a hole in the dirt. They stared at The Powerpuff Girls with their shiny red eyes.

"I think they're going to attack!" yelled Buttercup.

"Maybe I can talk to them," Bubbles suggested.

"But, we don't have time to fight *or* talk to a bunch of moles," moaned Blossom. "We've got to find Petunia."

If Bubbles decides to reason with the moles, turn to page 38.

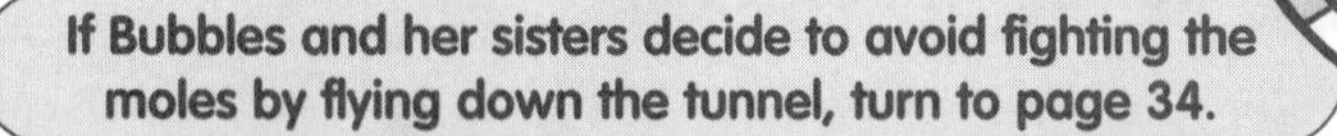

If Bubbles and her sisters decide to avoid fighting the moles by flying down the tunnel, turn to page 34.

"Let's see if Princess is home," said Bubbles. She pressed the button on the security gate.

Princess's face appeared on a video screen next to the buzzer. She wore a gold crown in her frizzy red hair. She scowled when she saw The Powerpuff Girls.

"What do you want?" she snapped.

"We're looking for Petunia the elephant," Bubbles said. "Do you know where she is?"

"I don't know any Petunia," said Princess. "But I saw an elephant in the park a little while ago. So why don't you scram?"

The video screen went black.

If Bubbles believes Princess and The Powerpuff Girls go to the park, turn to page 22.

If Bubbles and her sisters decide to blast their way into Princess's mansion, turn to page 28.

"Let's blast our way in!" cried Buttercup.

Blossom and Bubbles agreed.

The Girls combined their laser eye beam power. Pink laser eye beams came out of Blossom's eyes, blue laser eye beams came out of Bubbles's eyes, and green laser eye beams came out of Buttercup's eyes. The three sets of eye beams quickly blasted a hole through Princess's gate and melted the outdoor security system. The Girls knew that the Morbucks mansion was so huge that Princess was unlikely to hear the blast. The sisters zoomed through the front door.

"Where do we start?" Blossom wondered.

Then Bubbles heard a far-off noise.

"That sounds like an elephant," Bubbles said. "Let's follow it!"

The Girls flew down one long hallway after another until they entered a giant room. Gold cages filled the room, and each cage contained a different animal. One cage held an ostrich. One cage held a chattering monkey. A zebra munched on grass in another cage. And the largest cage of all had Petunia!

Bubbles flew to Petunia's cage. "We'll save you," she told the elephant.

"That's what you think!" said a whiny voice.

Bubbles spun around. A giant gold robot stomped into the indoor zoo. Princess sat inside the robot's head, controlling its moves.

"My zoo needs an elephant," Princess said. "I'm not giving her back. And you can't make me!"

If Bubbles attacks the robot with a laser blast, turn to page 39.

If Bubbles uses a super-kick, turn to page 40.

"I don't think we should leave the circus yet," said Bubbles. "Maybe some of the other animals can help us."

"I guess you're right," Buttercup said. "We can use all the help we can get!"

The Girls flew around the tents, looking for more animals to question. Then Bubbles spotted three fluffy white poodles walking by. Each poodle wore a frilly red collar and a tiny clown hat.

"*Hello,*" Bubbles said in poodle language. "*We are trying to find out what happened to Petunia. Can you help us?*"

The poodles wagged their tails.

"*Sure,*" said the first poodle. "*Petunia has been very sad lately. We think maybe she went someplace that would cheer her up.*"

"*She likes little kids,*" said the second poodle.

"*And she loves to eat,*" piped up the third poodle.

"*Thanks,*" said Bubbles. She told her sisters what the poodles had said.

"Where should we check first?" asked Blossom.

If Bubbles and her sisters decide to go to Pokey Oaks Kindergarten, turn to page 42.

If Bubbles and her sisters decide to go to the supermarket, because that's where you might go if you love to eat, turn to page 44.

"I believe them for once," Bubbles said. "This mess is too much, even for the Gangreen Gang. Let's go find Petunia!"

Buttercup looked at Ace with narrowed eyes. "All right," she said. "But if we find out you goons were lying, we're coming back for you!"

The Girls followed Big Billy's directions and took off. They floated along the trail of squashed bushes, flowers, and picnic baskets.

"*Petunia!*" Bubbles called out. "*Petunia, are you there?*"

Soon the trail came to an end. There were two ways to go. One path led away from the park, toward the waterfront. Another path led into the woods.

"Oh, no!" wailed Bubbles. "Which way did Petunia go?"

If Bubbles and her sisters follow the path to the waterfront, turn to page 47.

If Bubbles and her sisters go into the woods, turn to page 48.

"You must know something, Mojo," Bubbles said. "Are you sure you didn't see Petunia anywhere?"

"You did not ask me that," said Mojo Jojo. "You asked me if there was an elephant in my observatory. Which there is not. But I did see an elephant heading down to the waterfront when I was spy—er, observing the people of Townsville earlier today."

"Thanks, Mojo," said Bubbles. She turned to her sisters. "Come on. Let's go to the waterfront."

Before she left, Buttercup looked at Mojo. She pounded her fists together. "If we find out you were lying, we're coming back for you!"

Continue on page 47.

"All right," said Bubbles, "let's see where this tunnel leads."

The Girls flew farther into the dark tunnel.

Then Bubbles noticed something gleam overhead. She stopped.

"Hey, look at this!" she told her sisters.

There was a metal trapdoor overhead. Together, Blossom, Bubbles, and Buttercup used their superstrength to lift up the trapdoor. Bright light hit their eyes.

Bubbles blinked. They were inside a large room filled with gold cages. Each cage was filled with a different animal. And there, in the largest cage, was Petunia!

But there was more. A big gold robot was stomping across the room. Inside the robot was a girl with frizzy red hair—Princess Morbucks! She sat inside the robot's head, controlling the robot with a joystick and a panel of buttons.

Princess Morbucks was a very spoiled little girl. She believed she was entitled to whatever she wanted—whether it belonged to her or not. The Powerpuff Girls had defeated her before. But Princess was always looking for ways to get the best of the Girls.

"Thanks to my new robot, nobody will be able to take my new prize elephant away from me!" Princess said gleefully.

Bubbles realized that Princess hadn't seen them yet.

"This is our chance," Bubbles whispered to her sisters. "We can save Petunia!"

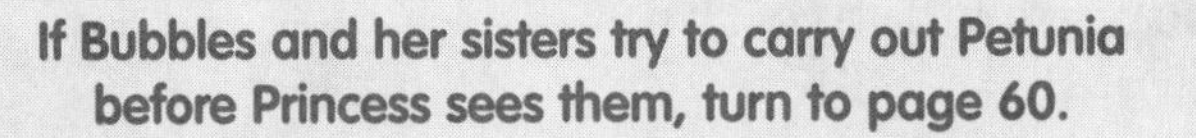

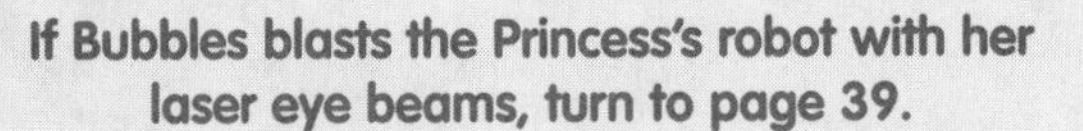

Ace made Bubbles angry.

"This park belongs to everybody," Bubbles said.

"Let's get 'em!" cried Blossom.

Pow! Buttercup hit Snake with a power punch.

Bam! Blossom sidelined Ace with a super-kick.

Wham! Buttercup picked up Little Arturo and sent him soaring into the swing set.

Whack! Blossom used another super-kick on Grubber.

That left one member of the Gangreen Gang to go.

Slam! Bubbles sent Big Billy flying with a power punch. Then something strange happened. Big Billy seemed to hit something in midair. Then he slid down to the grass—and disappeared into the ground!

"Huh?" Bubbles flew to Big Billy. He had crashed into a clear plastic wall and then fallen into a hole in the ground. It looked like some kind of booby trap! Bubbles peered into the darkness and saw an underground tunnel.

"This is really suspicious," Bubbles said. "I wonder where that tunnel leads to?"

Continue on page 18.

"*Wait!*" Bubbles cried. "*We don't want to fight you, moles. I'm sorry if we made you mad.*"

"*Nobody likes us,*" said the first mole sadly. "*They hate us because we are mutants. We have to live underground so nobody will bother us.*"

Then Bubbles had an idea.

"*I know someplace where people will be happy to see you,*" she told them. "*Follow us!*"

The Powerpuff Girls took the moles back to the circus grounds. Fred Friendly was astonished at the sight of the giant moles.

"They'll make a great circus act," Fred said.

The moles squeaked and cheered.

"But we still haven't found Petunia yet," said Bubbles.

Fred Friendly smiled. "I almost forgot. Petunia came back a little while ago. She had just been taking a stroll around Townsville after all!"

"Hooray! I'm so happy! Now the circus can go on!" cheered Bubbles.

Continue on page 64.

Bubbles started the attack on Princess's giant robot. Blue laser eye beams shot out of her eyes.

Zap! Blossom joined in with pink laser eye beams.

Zap! Buttercup's green laser eye beams completed the attack.

Normally, nothing could withstand a triple laser eye beam blast from The Powerpuff Girls. But the robot didn't seem affected.

Inside the robot, Princess laughed.

"I knew you would try to stop me," she said. "So I got Daddy to buy me this laser-absorbing robot. It absorbs your loser lasers and drains your energy at the same time!"

Bubbles knew Princess wasn't lying. She felt weak, like something had knocked the wind out of her.

There had to be some way to defeat Princess!

If Bubbles tries another laser attack, turn to page 63.

If Bubbles asks Petunia for help, turn to page 19.

"Petunia isn't yours!" Bubbles yelled. "She belongs in the circus!"

Bubbles whizzed across the room, building up speed. Then...

Whack! She slammed into the robot with a super-kick.

"No fair!" whined Princess. The robot rocked back and forth. Princess looked panicked. She pressed every button on the control panel. It was no use.

"Noooo!" Princess cried. The robot toppled to the floor with a loud crash. Princess flew out of the robot and landed at Blossom's and Buttercup's feet. She tried to run away.

Blossom grabbed her. "Not so fast, Princess. I'm sure the police will want to hear all about how you kidnapped a poor defenseless elephant!"

"She's my elephant! Mine! Aren't you, Petunia?" Princess asked.

Petunia snorted. "*No way,*" Petunia said. "*I'd never stay with anybody who kept me cooped up in a cage.*"

Bubbles grinned. "Petunia said she doesn't like being in a cage," Bubbles said. "And I bet you won't, either. We're calling the police!"

Bubbles flew to Petunia's cage and opened the door.

"*You're free, Petunia!*" Bubbles said happily. "*Let's get you back to the circus.*"

Continue on page 60.

"There are lots of kids at our school," said Bubbles. "Maybe Petunia went to Pokey Oaks."

"Let's go!" cried Blossom and Buttercup.

The Girls flew to the suburbs of Townsville. Pokey Oaks Kindergarten was a tiny brick building on a bright green lawn. Outside, the kids in their class were playing on the playground rides. And they weren't alone.

A big gray elephant was standing on the lawn. Elmer Sglue, one of the boys in their class, was swinging on the elephant's trunk.

"Look! It's Petunia!" Bubbles cried.

Continue on page 51.

Bubbles decided she and her sisters should follow Rainbow the Clown. That gold wrench might belong to Princess, but Rainbow was right in front of her. They couldn't just let him walk away.

"That's Rainbow the Clown," Bubbles whispered to her sisters. "Let's follow him. He might be up to something!"

The Girls secretly followed Rainbow as he left the circus grounds. The clown walked into the woods. Rainbow stepped into a clearing. And there, chained to a post, was Petunia!

"Rainbow! What are you doing with Petunia?" Bubbles asked.

Rainbow slumped at the sight of the Girls. "Ever since I got out of jail it's been hard for me to get work. I thought if I stole Petunia, I could start my own circus."

"Shame on you," said Blossom.

Bubbles released Petunia. "*Don't worry. We're taking you back to the circus,*" she told the elephant.

"And we're taking *you* back to jail!" Buttercup told Rainbow.

Continue on page 64.

"Let's try the supermarket," said Bubbles. "Maybe Petunia went there."

The Girls flew to the big supermarket on the edge of town. Shoppers were streaming out of the doors, screaming.

"It looks like something's going on here," Blossom said.

It didn't take them long to find Petunia. The elephant had knocked over aisles of food and was standing on a pile of crushed cartons, munching on peanuts. Her giant ears flapped happily as she ate.

The store manager approached the Girls, wringing his hands. "Thank goodness you're here," he said. "This elephant stomped in here a little while ago. She's been eating every peanut in sight. We can't budge her!"

"We'll talk to her," Bubbles reassured him. She turned to Petunia.

"They miss you at the circus, Petunia," Bubbles told the elephant. *"Please come with us."*

But Petunia didn't even answer. She just kept eating peanuts.

Blossom picked up an empty peanut bag.

"Hmmm," said Blossom. "These are Sunny Brand peanuts."

Something clicked in Bubbles's head. She knew what Blossom was thinking.

"Is this the only brand of peanuts Petunia has been eating?" Bubbles asked the store manager.

The man nodded. "As a matter of fact, yes," he said.

"Petunia, I think I know how to make you happy again," Bubbles said.

Continue on page 58.

Blossom, Bubbles, and Buttercup flew down to the waterfront. And sure enough, Petunia was there! The elephant was looking out over the water. She looked sad.

Bubbles flew up to Petunia's face. "*I'm Bubbles,*" she said. "*My sisters and I have been looking for you. Everyone at the circus is worried about you.*"

Petunia didn't answer. She just kept staring out at the water. Her large ears flapped gently in the breeze.

"*Why don't you come back with us?*" Bubbles asked.

Petunia sighed. "*I'm sorry,*" she said finally. "*It's just—*"

"*What's wrong?*" Bubbles wondered.

"*I used to live in a small cage in a zoo,*" Petunia said. "*It wasn't very nice. But I met some other elephants there. They told me all about Africa. That's where elephants like me come from, you know.*"

Bubbles nodded.

"*I can just imagine roaming across the beautiful African plains,*" Petunia said, closing her eyes. "*I would love to go there. Even just to visit.*"

Bubbles told her sisters what Petunia had said.

"That's so sad," said Blossom. Even Buttercup wiped a tear from her eye.

"Maybe we can help her," Buttercup said.

If Bubbles tries to find a boat headed for Africa to put Petunia on, turn to page 54.

If Bubbles and the other two Girls decide to help Petunia by first taking her back to the circus, turn to page 53.

"Let's try the woods," Bubbles suggested.

Blossom and Buttercup agreed. They flew into the woods and were able to find a trail of broken tree branches.

Soon they came to a clearing. There, sitting on an old log, was Petunia. The elephant looked glum.

Bubbles flew in front of Petunia's large face.

"*Hi there,*" she said. "*My name is Bubbles.*"

Petunia gave a little wave with her trunk. "*Nice to meet you,*" she replied. "*My name is Petunia.*"

"*We know,*" Bubbles said. "*Fred Friendly asked my sisters and me to look for you. Everyone at the circus is worried about you!*"

Petunia lowered her eyes. "*I don't want to go back there.*"

"*Why not?*" Bubbles asked. "*Are they mean to you?*"

Petunia shook her head. "*That's not it. I like everyone at the circus. I like Fred Friendly. But I don't like performing. I have stage fright!*"

Bubbles told her sisters what Petunia's problem was.

"An elephant with stage fright!" Blossom said. "Why didn't we think of that?"

Bubbles turned back to Petunia.

"*Don't worry,*" Bubbles said. "*We'll find a way to help you.*"

If Bubbles and her sisters promise to help Petunia back at the circus, turn to page 59.

If Bubbles finds another way to help Petunia, turn to page 56.

MITCH
ROCKS

Bubbles flew up to Petunia's face. "*Hi, Petunia,*" Bubbles said. "*My name is Bubbles.*"

"*Hi there,*" Petunia said. Her big blue eyes sparkled happily.

Petunia knelt down on the grass. Mitch Mitchelson and some other kids climbed on top of her back, while Julie Bean perched on the elephant's head. Petunia gracefully stood up and began to walk around the lawn.

Bubbles followed her. "*Petunia, everyone at the circus is worried about you. What are you doing here?*" she asked.

"*I can't help it,*" Petunia said. "*Before Fred Friendly rescued me, I worked at a carnival. I used to let children ride on my back. I don't miss the carnival, but I do miss the children.*"

"*But lots of children come to the circus,*" said Bubbles.

Petunia nodded. "*Yes, but I don't get to play with any of them. Now I just do my act. It's very lonely.*"

Bubbles told her sisters what the elephant had said. The Girls talked in a huddle.

"*We have an idea,*" Bubbles said. "*We think we can help you, Petunia.*"

If Bubbles tells their idea to help Petunia to their teacher, Ms. Keane, turn to page 52.

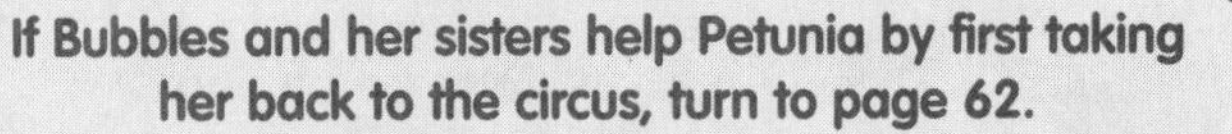

If Bubbles and her sisters help Petunia by first taking her back to the circus, turn to page 62.

Bubbles told her idea to keep Petunia to Ms. Keane. "If Petunia stays here, she can play with us at recess," Bubbles said. "And we can all learn about animals, too."

"That just might work, Bubbles," said Ms. Keane.

"Hooray!" cheered The Powerpuff Girls.

Petunia was thrilled by the news. She curled Bubbles in her trunk and raised her in the air. Bubbles giggled.

"*Thank you, Bubbles,*" said Petunia, after she put Bubbles back on the ground. "*But what will I tell Fred Friendly?*"

"*Don't worry,*" Bubbles told her. "*We'll take care of it.*"

The Girls flew back to the circus and told Fred Friendly what had happened.

"I don't want Petunia to be unhappy," Fred said. "I'll just have to find another star act. Lenny the Lion has been working hard on his act. Maybe he can be the new star of the show."

"I bet he'd like that," said Bubbles.

Continue on page 64.

"*We'll talk to Fred Friendly,*" Bubbles told Petunia. "*We'll make sure you get to see Africa.*"

Petunia let the Girls use their super-strength to carry her back to the circus. Fred Friendly ran right up and gave Petunia a big hug.

"I'm so glad you're safe!" Fred said.

Bubbles explained why Petunia had run away. Fred scratched his head for a bit. Then he smiled.

"Petunia, how would you like to spend the summer in Africa when the circus season is over?" he asked. "You deserve a vacation. And if you like it there, you're free to stay."

Petunia raised her trunk and gave a happy roar. Then she turned to Bubbles.

"*Thank you, Bubbles,*" she said.

Bubbles smiled. "*No problem, Petunia!*"

Continue on page 64.

Bubbles searched the waterfront until she found a ship headed for Africa. When she told the ship captain Petunia's story, he was happy to help.

Petunia's eyes filled with tears as she boarded the boat. "*Thank you so much, Bubbles,*" Petunia said. "*I will never forget you!*"

The Girls waved good-bye as the boat sailed out of the harbor.

"We made Petunia happy," Bubbles said. "Isn't that great?"

"I bet Fred Friendly won't be happy," Blossom said. "The star act for his circus is on a boat to Africa!"

"Oh, no!" wailed Bubbles. "I forgot about that!"

"Did somebody say circus?"

The Girls spun around. The Talking Dog was walking along the waterfront. The white dog was like any other dog, except he could speak perfect English.

"I love the circus," chattered the Talking Dog. "Do you know where I can get tickets? I would love to go. I love the acrobats. I love the cotton candy. I love the clowns..."

As the Talking Dog gabbed on, Bubbles had an idea. The Girls took the Talking Dog to see Fred Friendly. Bubbles told Mr. Friendly what had happened with Petunia.

"Wouldn't the Talking Dog make a great star attraction for your circus?" Bubbles suggested.

"Me? A star?" said the Talking Dog, grinning happily. "Imagine that!"

"I love it!" said Fred Friendly. "Thanks, Bubbles!"

Continue on page 64.

"*You shouldn't have to perform if you are scared,*" Bubbles told Petunia. "*I think I know a place where you can stay.*"

The Girls used their super-strength to fly Petunia to the Mayor's office. Bubbles told the Mayor her idea.

"You have lots of room here," Bubbles said. "Petunia could keep you company. She can water the grass. And she would make a beautiful fountain for the front lawn."

"An elephant! Oh, boy," said the Mayor. "I've wanted an elephant ever since I was a little tyke. And the front lawn is starting to look a little brown. Petunia can stay as long as she likes."

Petunia smiled. "*Thank you. I know I will like it here!*" she said.

"That takes care of Petunia," said Blossom. "But what will the circus do without her?"

"Oh, no!" wailed Bubbles. "I forgot about that. Mayor, we have to go."

The Girls flew back to the circus. They told Fred Friendly what had happened.

"I didn't realize Petunia was so unhappy," Fred said. "I feel terrible. But I'm glad she is happy with the Mayor."

"But what will you do for a star act?" Buttercup asked.

"Lenny the Lion loves the spotlight," Fred said. "He'll be thrilled if I make him the star of the show."

"Yay! It's a happy ending," cheered Bubbles.

Continue on page 64.

"*Your trainer Barney changed your peanuts from Sunny Brand to Nutty Brand,*" Bubbles said. "*I bet you miss Sunny Brand peanuts. Is that why you're here?*"

Petunia nodded. "*Finally, someone who understands me!*" she said. "*Nutty Brand peanuts just aren't as yummy and crunchy as Sunny Brand.*"

"*I'm sure Barney will understand,*" Bubbles said. "*Come on, let's go talk to him.*"

The Girls used their super-strength to carry Petunia back to the circus. They set her down gently in front of Barney's trailer. The trainer looked thrilled to see her.

"Petunia! You're back!" he cried happily. "I missed you so much."

Bubbles explained why Petunia ran away.

"Petunia, I'm so sorry," Barney said. "I promise I'll switch back to Sunny Brand peanuts. And I'll never switch brands on you again!"

Petunia lifted up her trunk and gave a happy roar.

Just then, Fred Friendly ran up. Barney and the Girls told him what had happened.

"Thanks for helping Petunia, Girls!" Fred Friendly said. "The circus is about to start," he said. "Let's get ready for the show!"

Continue on page 64.

"*I have an idea,*" Bubbles said to Petunia. "*Come back to the circus with us and I'll help you get over your stage fright. If you're still scared, we'll talk to Fred Friendly.*"

Petunia sighed. "*Okay. I'll give it a try.*"

The Girls used their super-strength to fly Petunia back to the circus. They got back just in time for Petunia to do her act.

Barney, Petunia's trainer, gave her a big hug. "Oh, Petunia! I'm so glad you're back. Are you ready to go on?"

Petunia looked at Bubbles.

"*Don't worry,*" Bubbles said. "*I'll be with you the whole time.*"

And she was. Bubbles flew next to Petunia's ear while she did her act. She whispered words of encouragement to the elephant. With Bubbles's help, Petunia bounced a basketball with her trunk. She played a song on a xylophone. Petunia ended by dancing a two-step.

The crowd went wild. Petunia blushed.

"*You did it!*" Bubbles said.

"*I know,*" Petunia said. "*And it was kind of fun this time. I think I'll be able to do my act from now on—thanks to you. I never could have done it without you, Bubbles!*"

Continue on page 64.

The Girls used their super-strength to carry Petunia out of her cage and back to the circus. Bubbles heard Princess screaming behind them.

"Petunia is my elephant. Mine, mine, mine!" Princess screeched.

The Girls flew until they saw the colorful tents of the circus below them. They gently set Petunia down in front of the largest tent—the Big Top.

The circus animals cheered when they saw Petunia. Fred Friendly ran out of the Big Top in his bright orange suit. He gave Petunia a big hug.

"I'm so glad you're safe, Petunia," Fred said. "Powerpuff Girls, I can't thank you enough."

"How about front row seats?" Buttercup suggested.

"Sure, you got it," said Fred. "We'd better hurry. It's almost show time!"

Continue on page 64.

"*Let's go talk to Fred Friendly,*" Bubbles said to Petunia. "*I'm sure he'll understand.*"

Petunia agreed, and the Girls used their super-strength to carry the elephant back to the circus. They set Petunia down in front of the largest circus tent. Fred Friendly broke into a big smile when he saw Petunia.

"I'm so glad you're back!" he said. "What happened?"

Bubbles explained why Petunia had run away. Then she told Fred her idea.

"Why don't you let Petunia play with the children who come see the circus?" Bubbles suggested. "She can play with them outside the main tent before every show."

"That's a great idea!" Fred said. "As long as it makes you happy, Petunia."

Petunia lifted up her trunk and gave a happy roar.

"*Thank you, Bubbles,*" Petunia said. "*I'll never be lonely again!*"

Continue on page 64.

"One...more...blast..." Bubbles said weakly.

Bubbles used her last ounce of strength to aim a laser eye beam at the robot.

The beam whizzed right past the robot without making contact.

"Ha!" said Princess. "You'll never beat me—"

Whoo-oop! Whoo-oop! Whoo-oop!

"Oh, no!" wailed Princess. "The indoor security system!"

"What luck, Bubbles!" exclaimed Blossom. "Your laser eye beam must have hit the security system when it missed the robot. The police will be here in seconds."

Soon sirens filled the air. The Powerpuff Girls quickly regained their strength.

Bam! Bang! Zoom! They couldn't use their laser eye beams, but their super-strength took down the giant hunk of metal in seconds flat.

The Girls pried Princess out of the robot and held her until the police arrived. Then they used their super-strength to release Petunia from her cage and carry her back to the circus.

Every clown, acrobat, and trained animal cheered as The Powerpuff Girls gently set Petunia on the circus grounds. Fred Friendly gave Petunia a big hug.

"Thank you so much, Powerpuff Girls," said Fred. "You've saved the circus!"

Continue on page 64.

"We did it!" Bubbles said happily.

Bubbles felt great.

Petunia was happy.

Fred Friendly was happy.

And The Powerpuff Girls were happy, too. They all got front row seats for the big show!

So once again, the day is saved (and so is Petunia), thanks to The Powerpuff Girls—and Fred Friendly's Circus!

THE END